AGENT ALFIE
LICENCE TO FISH

Justin Richards

Illustrations by Jim Hansen

HarperCollins *Children's Books*

First published in Great Britain by HarperCollins Children's Books 200?

HarperCollins Children's Books is a division of
HarperCollinsPublishers Ltd
77-85 Fulham Palace Road, Hammersmith, London W6 8JB

The HarperCollins Children's Books website address is
www.harpercollinschildrensbooks.co.uk

1

Text copyright © Justin Richards 2009

Justin Richards asserts the moral right to be identified
as the author of this work

ISBN 978-0-00-727359-1

Printed and bound in England by
Clays Ltd, St Ives plc

To Alison, who keeps the young agents

under control. Sometimes.

Welcome to Thunder Raker Manor

An Introduction to the School
by Mr Trenchard, Head Teacher

Thunder Raker Manor is an exclusive school
for boys and girls from 8 to 18. Some of the
children come daily, some are boarders. Some
of them I remember, some of them I— er,
what was I saying?

Anyway, all our students are here because
their parents or guardians are connected
with the Security Services. Spies and agents
are happy to send their children to Thunder
Raker Manor secure in the knowledge that
they will be safe from any possible threats.

We teach a full curriculum at Thunder
Raker, fully compliant with the National
Thingummy. And alongside the English and
Maths and History and Geography, our
students learn skills that may just come in
handy back home or in their future careers

— if they have inherited their parents'
inclinations and aptitudes.

As well as being an honorary CT (Classified
Training) Academy, Thunder Raker is
especially pleased with its latest SATS
results. We take the Special Agent Training
Standards very seriously indeed and have
achieved excellent levels in Surveillance,
Code Breaking and Sabotage.

And if the Security Services need a bit of
help from some youngsters for a special
mission, or if the villainous agents of that
dastardly organisation known only as the
Secret Partners for Undertaking Destruction
(SPUD) try to take over the school or kidnap
one of the teachers — rest assured, every
one of our students is ready and prepared.

*Mr Trenchard has been the Head Teacher of
Thunder Raker Manor since Mrs Muldoom's
unfortunate accident on the assault course
all those years ago. He is superbly qualified
and takes great pride in his work. When he
can remember what it is. Very good — carry
on. Um. Yes...*

Mr Trenchard

Colonel Hugh Dare-Swynne's Class of the Week
This week the Colonel focuses on Class 3D, which is taught by Miss Jones.

Miss Jones

Miss Jones says:

3D is a lovely class and works hard. This year was especially exciting for everyone as we had a new student start — Alfie (surname classified). Alfie is already settling in very well, and even has his own cover story — some nonsense about his father actually being a postman.
As if!

Alfie

Alfie fits in well with the other children. He is nine years old, and he's a clever, practical boy with lots of common sense. He's brave and loyal and fun. Though I have to say he doesn't always quite understand some of the lessons or the way we do things here at Thunder Raker. But his common sense approach is a breath of fresh air and he sees the world — and our problems — in a much less cluttered and complicated way than the other children.

Jack

Next up is Jack. Jack's dad is head of the Secret Service, though of course we don't mention that. But it does explain why Jack's a bit full of himself. He is always coming up with terrific ideas and plans, though usually they are rather impractical and just too involved ever to work.

Harry

Harry's dad has infiltrated SPUD and
sends him strange, coded text messages
and letters written in invisible ink.
Sometimes the children have to go and
rescue or help him, which cuts into the
school day. Harry isn't the brightest of
the bunch by a long way, but his
questions often throw up problems with
Jack's ideas. He is brave and loyal and
willing and likes doing PE — on the
school assault course.

Sam

Sam's mum works in Whitehall for
Hush Hush, designing equipment for
agents and spies. Sam uses a
motorised wheelchair — which looks
ordinary but has amazing gadgets
built into it. Sam's mum made him
his wheelchair because the NHS
one didn't have a very good
anti-missile protection system.
And one of the wheels was wonky.

Chloe

Moving on to the girls, Chloe is the
daughter of a renowned spy (and
doesn't she know it). If you thought
Jack was a bit full of himself, he's
got nothing on Chloe. She just has to
be the centre of attention, wearing
the latest fashion — and spying —
accessories. At home she's got her
telly wired up with a Playstation 3,
a Wii, and the very latest
omni-processing decryptortron.
Unfortunately Alfie isn't terribly
impressed by all this, so he and Chloe
haven't really hit it off.

Alice

Alice's dad is a double agent (but
it's a bit unclear which side
he's actually on). You never know
where you are with Alice — she
says one thing then does another.
Her moods are volatile and she's
got a temper like a tank-buster
missile when it goes off.

Beth

Beth is a swot and a techie. Her dad is a
super-boffin who runs the Government's
Inventing Taskforce (GIT). She's inherited
his absented-minded braininess. She's not
so hot on the practical side of things
though — she can design a robot to tie your
shoelaces, but she's always tripping over
her own feet. She comes to school on her
rocket-powered rollerblades.

A Passion for Excellence

Miss Jones

Miss Jones is responsible for teaching
Class 3D the ordinary everyday subjects
like Maths and English and History. She's
newly qualified, quiet and unassuming.
Like Miss Jones, all the subject teachers
at Thunder Raker Manor are fully
qualified and at the very peak of their
profession. Many of them are former
agents and spies, so together they bring
a wealth of experience to the school.

Mr Cryption

Mr Cryption teaches Codes.
He's tall and thin and no one
understands anything he says.

Miss Fortune

Miss Fortune teaches Assassination. Her classes always seem to be a few pupils short — they get sent on errands or asked to help fetch something, and never come back... Note, though, that Class 3D is too young for Assassination, which is only taught in the Sixth Form.

Sir Westerly Compass

Sir Westerly Compass is in charge of Tracking Skills. He's always late for class, and his lessons are often moved at short notice.

The Major

The Major — that's all he's ever called — is in charge of Sabotage Training. He has an enormous moustache and he's rather accident prone. Everything he touches breaks — even the plate he gets his school dinner on...

Mrs Nuffink

Mrs Nuffink teaches Surveillance. Don't mess around in her class — she's got eyes in the back of her head. No, really.

Mr Trick

Camouflage is supposed to be taught by Mr Trick. But no one can find him.

Reverend "Bongo" Smithers

The Chaplain is Reverend "Bongo" Smithers, a former fighter pilot more interested in war stories than Bible stories. He also teaches PE. Ruthlessly.

Top Secret

Peace of Mind

So whatever your parental requirements or security clearance, you can rest assured that Thunder Raker Manor will provide a first-class education for your child in every respect. We can't tell you how much the children enjoy being here. No, really — we can't. It's an official secret.

Chapter I

It was still quite dark when Alfie walked to school, but the men watching him from the hedges and ditches all wore sunglasses. This meant they had trouble seeing Alfie, and had to lean right out from their hiding places. Then they'd suddenly pull back into hiding when he got too close. Alfie ignored them and kept going.

He might have felt sorry for them, stuck out in the cold and the wet all night, except for two things. First, Alfie knew that they were agents of SPUD – the Secret Partners for Undertaking Destruction. They were spying on Alfie and all the other pupils and staff at Thunder Raker Manor School. And the second thing was that Alfie knew Mrs Prendergast would soon come out from her little cottage to offer them tea and biscuits.

Alfie was early this morning because he wanted to get to school in time to ask one of his friends about his homework. It had been set by Mr Cryption the Codes teacher, and Alfie didn't really understand what he was supposed to do. He had been given a sheet of lined paper, with a heading at the top. There was no explanation, and the heading simply asked, 'Extraction Luggage Mangle?'.

So Alfie ignored the SPUD agents, and made his way up to the main school gates. He said hello to Sergeant Custer, who was on guard as usual. He paused to pat Gerald the guard dog. Then he made his way up the school drive and was soon in his classroom.

Only one of Alfie's friends from Class 3D had arrived before him. It was Jack. His dad was head of the Secret Service, which sounded very exciting. In fact, all the children at Thunder

Raker had parents or guardians who were in the Secret Service, or were spies or agents. All except Alfie.

His dad was a postman.

Everyone else thought this was great cover, and only Alfie knew he was at Thunder Raker because there had been a mistake. But Alfie loved the school and all his classmates, so he never said anything or complained.

"Hi, Alfie," said Jack. "Did you get the Codes homework done, then?"

"I didn't really understand the question," Alfie confessed.

"Not surprised," said Jack. "Have you heard about the new fishing club?"

"That's it?" said Alfie. "Strange homework question."

He got his homework out of his backpack, and wrote carefully under the heading: 'No, I haven't heard about the new fishing club'. He thought for a moment, and then added neatly: 'Fester scribble'.

"What are you doing?" Jack asked as he watched Alfie write.

"Answering the question."

"Great." Jack pulled out his own homework sheet. It was as blank as Alfie's had been. 'So, what is it?"

Alfie frowned. "Have you heard about the new fishing club?"

"How strange," said Jack. "I just asked you the same thing. And the notice only went up this morning, so I'm surprised Mr Cryption knew about it."

Alfie was beginning to think that maybe he had misunderstood. But the other children in Class 3D were arriving now.

"What's that about a fishing club?" Alice asked. "I think fishing is cruel to fish."

"Perhaps they can join too," said Jack. "Sounds a bit boring though."

Sam rolled up in his wheelchair. "Maybe I can get a special fishing attachment." His

wheelchair was packed with gadgets and defensive equipment. "That would make it more fun."

Jack said something in reply, but his words were drowned out by the noise of Beth arriving – on a rocket-powered scooter. She was wearing a bright pink crash helmet, and stopped so suddenly beside her desk that the crash helmet kept going. It flew across the room and hit Harry as he came through the door.

"Oof," he said, and doubled over.

"Do stand up straight, Harry," Chloe said, stepping into the classroom past him. "And give Beth back her helmet. Though I have to say it's a bit old-fashioned. Pink is *so* last week."

"Have you heard about the new fishing club?" Jack asked Harry.

"Fishing club?" Harry looked confused. "What do you do – hit them over the head with it?"

"Not that sort of club," Alfie said.

"I've got a golf club," Chloe said. "My dad gave it to me. There are eighteen holes in it and lots of famous people play golf there."

"Even though there are holes in it?" Harry asked.

"You don't go fishing with a club," Sam explained to Harry.

"That's right," Chloe said, taking back her pink crash helmet. "You go with a rod."

Harry was still looking perplexed. "Who's Rod?"

"Maybe he runs the club," Alice suggested.

"Some people go fishing with a net," Jack

pointed out. "That would have holes in."

Harry sat down heavily. "Who's Annette?!"

"Must be a friend of Rod," Chloe told him.

Luckily, Miss Jones the class teacher arrived before Harry got any more confused.

"Good morning, everyone," she said. "Now, before we go to Assembly, I have a message from Mr Cryption. He's very sorry that the homework he set you for last night didn't really make sense and he's asked me to apologise."

"Extraction Luggage Mangle," Sam muttered.

"I knew it couldn't be *that* easy."

"Yes," Miss Jones went on, "in fact, the question should have been…" She paused to check on a piece of paper. "Ah yes, here we are, it should have been: 'Igloo pest under armada brackets?'"

Sam slapped his palm to his forehead. "Of course!"

"But what does it mean?" Alfie whispered to him.

"Haven't a clue," Sam said. "I just put my answer as '167 Wednesdays'. I don't think I'll bother to change it."

Assembly started in the usual way, with the Head Teacher Mr Trenchard forgetting why everyone was there or what was going on. Years

ago, Mr Trenchard had trained himself to forget anything that might be useful to the enemy if he was captured. But now he seemed just to forget everything. All the time.

Eventually he remembered what the Assembly was about, and explained the plans for the day ahead.

"And finally," Mr Trenchard said, reading from his notes, "we have a new after-school club starting this week. The Fishing Club. There's already been a lot of interest, so each class will be allocated a day when they can go to the club. Today that class will be 3D."

"Oh how boring," Jack said. "I'm not going."

"Nor me," Beth agreed.

Sam shook his head too.

But Mr Trenchard hadn't finished. "Because the timetable is already so crowded, I'm afraid that anyone who does join the Fishing Club will have to miss the last lesson of the day. Which for Class 3D today would be..." he paused to check on a piece of paper, "...Political Destabilisation, with the Chaplain."

"I think fishing is way cool!" Jack said.

"Fishing Club – can't wait," Sam whispered.

"I'm there," Beth agreed.

"It's cruel to fish," Alice muttered.

Mr Trenchard was explaining which day each of the other classes could go fishing and what lessons they would miss. "You will meet by the school lake at the start of the last lesson. Any questions?"

The other teachers all sat on the stage beside Mr Trenchard. Alfie had noticed that there was always an empty chair on the end of the line. Beside the empty chair was the Major. He was in charge of sabotage training. "One thing," he said gruffly. He struggled to remain upright as a leg fell off his chair. "Who will be running this Fishing Club?"

"Ah, very good question." Mr Trenchard paused as the Major's chair toppled sideways and tipped him off the stage. "We have two experts coming in from the Advanced Fish Inspection Board."

"That's AFIB," the Chaplain announced, in case there was any confusion.

"No, no," Mr Trenchard insisted. "It's absolutely true."

"Experts!" Harry whispered to Alfie, obviously impressed.

"And their names," Mr Trenchard announced, "are Rod and Annette."

Chapter 2

The first lesson was Surveillance, with Mrs Nuffink. But it was clear that Class 3D was more excited by the thought of fishing than by watching grainy black and white CCTV footage of a supermarket car park.

"There!" Mrs Nuffink exclaimed in exasperation. "Did none of you see that?"

"See what?" Chloe asked.

"It was just a woman pushing a trolley," said Jack.

"A woman in dark glasses and combat gear," Alfie added.

"And what did you notice about the trolley?" Mrs Nuffink demanded.

They all looked at her blankly. "I've got better wheels?" Sam suggested.

"*Inside* the trolley?" Mrs Nuffink prompted. "Didn't you see anything worrying?"

"Groceries," Jack said.

"Frozen peas," Harry suggested.

Ideas came thick and fast now:

"Meat."

"Carrots."

"Books."

"A set of matching saucepans."

"A gorilla."

"*A gorilla*?!"

"Why not?"

"Fish."

"A rod and a net. Ha ha – only kidding, Harry."

Mrs Nuffink sighed. She adjusted a control on the video player and the image of the trolley froze, then zoomed in.

"There – look!"

"Oh," said Alfie.

"Ah," Alice exclaimed.

"It's a surface-to-air missile," Beth said. "Heat seeking, with dual-stage ignition and anti-wobble stabilisers."

"I didn't know they sold those down the supermarket," said Jack.

"That's because you never help with the shopping," Alice told him.

"Well," said Mrs Nuffink with satisfaction as she let the video play through, "isn't that a bit of a worry?"

"Not really," said Beth. "You can't launch those from inside a trolley."

The image on the screen juddered as the trolley hurtled rapidly towards the camera, trailing flames and smoke behind it.

The screen went white.

"See what I mean?" said Beth.

"I really don't think any of you have been paying full attention today," Mrs Nuffink said as she handed out homework sheets.

"We're excited about the Fishing Club," Harry explained.

"I cannot think why. Everyone knows the best way to catch fish is to lie in wait. Be patient. Watch and wait for the fish to appear."

"And then?" Chloe asked.

"Hit it with a club."

All the teachers seemed to have different ideas about how to catch fish. In PE, the Chaplain paused in his description of how to crawl under the automated machine guns and avoid the marauding lions to suggest gelignite.

"Gelignite?" said Beth. "But that's a powerful explosive."

The Chaplain nodded. "Just chuck it in the water. The shock wave from the explosion kills the fish and they float to the surface."

"Not much skill in that is there?" said Jack.

"Kill not skill," the Chaplain barked. "Anyway, with fish it isn't the skill that counts. With fish it's the scale. Now where were we? Oh yes, I was going to tell you about the hidden bear pit." He paused for a moment before saying to Alfie, "Just help Harry out of there, will you? Before Grizzly gets him. Thank you."

In Sabotage, the Major said he also had a good way to catch fish. But they never found out what it was, because at that moment he fell out of the window. Then through the skylight into the dining room.

He landed in a trough of baked beans.

Class 3D ran to the window and looked down at the mess.

"Someone should fish him out," said Alfie.

As soon as lessons were over, Class 3D hurried down to the lake at the back of the school. A man and a woman were waiting for them.

"You must be Class 3D," the man said. He was holding a fishing rod.

"We're very pleased to meet you," the woman said. She was holding a net.

They were both wearing business suits and dark glasses.

"They don't look much like people who go fishing," Jack said quietly.

"They look more like SPUD agents," Beth whispered.

"So," the man said, "I'm Rod Boiled."

The woman smiled. "And I'm Annette Mash."

As most of Class 3D had expected, fishing turned out to be rather boring. Rod gave a quick description of the fishing rod and the net and the various other pieces of equipment like floats and flies and reels and lines. Then Annette handed out rods and everyone practised casting their lines into the lake.

"If anyone catches a fish, they're in big trouble," said Alice. She had her arms folded and was refusing to join in.

"I don't know why you came," Jack told her.

"To protect the fish."

"It's all right," said Annette. "If we catch any

fish, we throw them straight back into the water."

"So what's the point?" Sam asked.

"They'll have holes in," said Harry. "Where the hook got them. Won't they leak and sink?"

"Fish sink anyway," said Chloe.

"How do we know if we've caught a fish?" Harry asked.

Annette's mobile phone was ringing and she turned away to answer it.

"You'll feel a tug on the rod," Rod said. "Then you know you've got a fish on the line."

Annette was holding out her phone to Rod. "I've got our boss on the line," she said.

Harry gasped in astonishment.

"That's nothing," Sam told him. "I heard there was a train on the line."

"He's just joking," Alfie assured Harry. "And I don't think we'll catch many fish anyway," he told Alice. "Not on our first day. And not without bait."

In fact, no one caught any fish at all. Soon it

was time to pack all the fishing gear away into the big bag that Rod and Annette had brought, and then go home.

Alfie was one of the last to leave. Rod and Annette were finishing tidying and putting things away. Alice was staring glumly into the lake, and Harry was tying his shoelace. It came undone again straight away.

"I'm sorry about the fish," said Alfie to Alice. "But I really don't think we'll catch very many, and Annette said we'll throw them all back. They'll be fine."

"Thanks," said Alice. "But I just don't think it's right to catch fish for no reason."

"We could eat them," said Harry. But that didn't seem to help. He gave up on his shoelaces and walked with Alice and Alfie back towards the school. "I had a fish as a pet once," he said.

"Really?" Alice asked.

"A goldfish."

"What was its name?" Alfie asked.

"Blue."

They walked a bit further, then Alice asked: "If it was a *gold*fish, why did you call it Blue?"

Harry seemed surprised at the question. "Because it *blew* bubbles," he said, as if this was obvious. "I have to go back to the classroom to get my backpack."

Alfie realised that he didn't have his backpack either. He'd taken it to Fishing Club, so he must have left it by the lake. He said goodbye to Alice and Harry and hurried back to get it.

He expected to meet Rod and Annette coming back towards the school, but there was no sign of them. The lake seemed calm and deserted. He wondered where they were. Alfie couldn't help thinking that they did look remarkably like SPUD agents. But why would an organisation like SPUD want to run fishing classes?

Alfie found his backpack where he had left it lying close to a bush. "There you are," said Alfie. "I'm glad I found you."

"I'm glad too," said a voice. "You must be Alfie."

Alfie stared. There was no one there. Just a bush.

"I think we need to have a little talk," said the bush. "There are some very strange things going on round here, I can tell you."

Alfie grabbed his bag, and ran.

Chapter 3

The next day before school, when Alfie told him about the talking bush, Jack thought it was the funniest thing he'd ever heard.

"Good one, Alfie. A talking bush! Tell Harry – he might even believe you."

"But it's true," Alfie protested. "This bush spoke to me."

"What, like, 'Give us a prune'?"

Harry arrived in time to hear this. "Do bushes eat prunes?" he wondered.

"Do bushes talk?" said Jack.

"That one down by the lake does," said Alfie. "I didn't imagine it."

Everyone was listening now. "I think Alfie's gone mad," Chloe said seriously. "He should be locked up in a secure place. For his own safety."

"What did this bush say to you?" Sam asked.

"It said there are some weird things going on."

"Like talking bushes," Beth agreed. "I think we should go and look."

"Go and listen, you mean," said Jack.

"We can go at break time," Alice suggested. "I want to look at the lake anyway, and check the Chaplain hasn't blown it up or anything."

At morning break, once Alice was satisfied that the lake wasn't covered in floating dead fish, they all gathered round the bush.

"Sure it was this one?" Beth asked.

"I'm sure," said Alfie. But now he was here again the whole idea just seemed silly. How could a bush *talk*?

"And it called

you by name?" Chloe said. "How

could it know your name?"

"It probably overheard us talking to Alfie

while we were fishing," Harry said.

Chloe stared at him. "It's a bush. Bushes

can't hear anything."

Jack was leaning against a nearby tree. "And

whoever heard of a talking bush?"

"Well," said the tree. "It's not that unusual,

actually."

Jack gave a shriek of surprise and leaped in

the air.

"Told you that bush couldn't talk," Chloe

said to Alfie. "It was the tree all the time."

"A talking tree?" said the tree in surprise.

"Where?"

"Er," Alfie said, "well you, really."

The tree laughed. Its branches shook and a few leaves fell off. "Whoever heard of a talking tree?"

Alfie and Beth looked at each other. Sam wheeled slightly closer, Harry and Jack close beside him. Alice and Chloe were looking rather puzzled.

"If you're not a talking tree,

what are you?" Alfie asked cautiously.

"Aliens," Jack said. "Got to be."

"My dad tried to invent an exploding horse chestnut tree once," Beth said. Her dad was an inventor with the Government Inventing Taskforce – known as GIT.

"What for?" Alice asked.

"To 'conker' the enemy."

Alfie was still waiting for an answer from the tree. "Well?" he prompted. "And how do you know my name?"

"I'm one of your teachers, so of course I know your name. I know all your names," said the tree.

"Of course!" Jack realised.

"Of course what?" said Alfie.

"Can't you see? This must be Mr Trick, the

camouflage teacher," explained Jack.

"Pleased to meet you all," said the tree.

"Sorry, sir," said Jack. "But what are you doing down here by the lake? Everyone's been looking for you."

"Not very hard, they haven't. And I'm on surveillance duty. Keeping an eye on the grounds. And as I told young Alfie here, there's something very odd going on."

"You're telling us," said Sam.

Then Mr Trick's voice came out of a nearby clump of stinging nettles: "I've been watching the lake," it said. "Keeping a look out for the huge, grey, long-necked monster that lives in the water."

There was an awkward pause. Then Chloe said in a hushed voice, "And I've been *fishing* in that!"

"It may have something to do with those two SPUD agents," Mr Trick's voice went on.

"Er – SPUD agents?" Jack asked.

"The ones who teach fishing," said Mr Trick.

The last lesson of the day was Tracking Skills. As usual, Sir Westerly Compass was not in his classroom. There was a note on the door sending 3D to room 14F.

"I didn't know there was a room 14F," said Jack.

"I think it's next to 9C," Beth told him.

"No, no," Chloe said. "That's 11Q. Or is it 2B?"

"2B or not 2B?" said Sam. "That is the question."

"The question is, do we believe in

monsters?" said Alfie. "We could spend the whole lesson searching for Sir Westerly Compass, like we usually do…"

"Or?" said Beth.

"Or we could go down to the lake before the Sixth Form have their Fishing Club. We could check up on Rod and Annette and see if they really are SPUD agents like Mr Trick said, and we could look for the monster."

"There is no monster," said Chloe. "And I think that Mr Trick was probably a… a trick. It was Alfie mucking about."

"No it wasn't," Alfie protested.

"Talking trees and bushes!" Chloe snorted.

"I think it's a great idea," Jack said. "SPUD spying and monster spotting. I'm in."

"I'm going to do my homework in the

library," Chloe decided.

"I'll go with Chloe," said Alice. "I don't want to be reminded that people catch fish – even SPUD people. Or that monsters might eat them. The fish, I mean. Not the SPUD agents."

"I ought to do some homework too," Sam said glumly. "I've got extra Sabotage Theory from the Major for mucking up my last test."

"What did you get wrong?" Alfie asked.

Sam shrugged. "Don't know. The Major gave me my test paper back, but someone had spilled coffee all over it and I couldn't read the teacher's comment. And it seemed to have caught fire."

"Well, I got 100 per cent, so I'm in," said Beth. "What about you, Harry?"

"If Rod and Annette are there, I might ask if I

can do some more fishing today," said Harry. "I
think I like it."

"He's hooked," said Sam, grinning.

On the way to the lake, Alfie, Harry, Beth and
Jack walked along the edge of the main playing
field. A little old lady was standing meekly in
the middle of a dozen sixth formers who were
lying flat on their backs groaning in pain.

One of the sixth formers struggled to his feet. Only to be knocked down again by a flying jump kick from the little old lady, accompanied by a fierce Ninja attack cry.

"I don't know if they'll be up to Fishing Club," said Jack. "Not after Assassination with Miss Fortune."

"If Rod and Annette are there, I'm definitely asking if I can do extra fishing," Harry said.

The sun was low in the sky, glinting on the surface of the lake. It made it difficult to see if there was a monster rising up from the water. But there was something – a huge, dark shape floating on the water.

"Duck!" Jack said.

Alfie, Harry and Beth ducked.

Jack stared at them in surprise. "No," he said,

urgently. "Big duck!"

They flung themselves to the ground.

Jack frowned. "There, in the lake." He pointed to the huge, dark shape. "There's a big duck in the lake."

From where he was now lying on the wet grass, Alfie could see that the shape was indeed a big duck. In fact, an enormous duck. It was about two metres tall. And bright yellow.

"You think that's the monster?" Beth asked.
"It's not grey."

"It's just a duck," Harry said.

"Big duck," Alfie pointed out.

"Don't you start," Beth said.

"I bet that's what Mr Trick saw," said Jack.
"He saw a big duck and thought it was a
monster."

Alfie wasn't convinced. "I don't think
a long-necked grey monster would
look like a big yellow duck."

"No," Harry agreed. "I think it would look more like that." He pointed at the lake.

Alfie and the others had to shield their eyes from the sun to see what he was pointing at.

It was an enormous, grey monster. Its long neck was rising up out of the water, in front of

the duck, looming over it – ready to strike. When the monster slowly sank out of sight, the duck was gone.

"Yes," Alfie said. "Exactly like that."

"Where did the duck go?" Beth asked.

"The monster ate it," said Jack. "Better not tell Alice!"

Harry was still shielding his eyes from the sun and looking down towards the edge of the lake. "There's Rod and Annette."

"Maybe they saw the duck and can tell us where it went," Alfie said. "Or the monster."

"I'm going to ask them," Harry decided. He ran off towards the lake shore.

The others waited as Harry spoke briefly to Rod and Annette – who were still both in their suits and dark glasses.

"You think they really are working for SPUD?" Beth asked.

"Got to be, dressed like that," Jack said confidently.

"Maybe," Alfie said. "They don't look like they usually teach fishing, do they? But if they're working for SPUD, what are they doing?"

"Spying on us," Jack said.

"Yeah, right," Beth told him. "They want to know how good we are at fishing. That'll help them in their plans."

"What are their plans?" Alfie wondered. "What does SPUD actually want, do you think?"

"Power," Jack told him. "They're always trying to rig elections and replace world leaders with their own agents."

"Loads of money," Beth added. "They rob banks and steal from wealthy countries."

"World domination," Jack said. "The usual."

Harry came running back, out of breath.

"Did you ask them?" Jack demanded. "What did they say?"

"They said I can do extra fishing on Thursday."

"So, you didn't ask if they saw the monster, then?" Alfie said.

"Or where that poor thing went?" Beth added.

"Where what poor thing went?"

"Duck, Harry!" Jack told him. "Big duck!"

"Get up, Harry," said Beth. "That's not what he meant."

Chapter 4

In morning break the next day, Beth unveiled her blueprint for a Monster Catcher. It was drawn on a large sheet of paper that covered several tables in the classroom. Everyone gathered round to see.

"It looks like Sam's wheelchair," said Alfie.

"That's because it *is* Sam's wheelchair," Beth explained.

"Sam's already got a wheelchair," said Chloe.

"I'm very happy with it," Sam agreed. "I don't need another one."

"It's Sam's wheelchair," said Beth, "with some special modifications."

"That looks like a big fishing rod," said Alice. She didn't sound happy about it.

"It's a rod for catching monsters." Beth

pointed to the blueprints. "This is actually thick rope instead of fishing line. This reel is made from an oil drum. The rod itself is a girder from the canteen roof. I've got all the bits ready and waiting to be put together."

"A girder from the canteen roof?" said Harry. "Doesn't the roof need it?"

"Don't be silly," Beth snapped. "I've already taken it down, and the roof is absolutely fine. So, if we're all agreed, I can weld everything together and attach it to Sam's chair at lunch time."

"If we can actually catch the monster," Alfie said, "then we might find out what's going on. Perhaps," he said as a thought occurred to him, "that's what Rod and Annette are here for. They're trying to catch the monster."

"In that case we need to catch it first," Beth said.

"Maybe we can go monster fishing in PE," said Alfie.

"Yeah, like the Chaplain will let us do that," Jack told him.

"Maybe we can persuade him," said Beth. "If we tell him that Rod and Annette are SPUD agents…"

"We don't have any proof of that, though," Alfie pointed out. "Just what Mr Trick said."

"We need to catch them in the act," Jack agreed.

"The act of what?" Alfie asked.

Discussions were interrupted by Miss Jones arriving at the end of break. "I'm glad you're all here and haven't gone off to your next lesson," she told Class 3D. "Lunch today will be in the school hall, and not in the canteen. There's some problem with the roof and the ceiling's fallen down."

"Nice one, Beth," said Jack quietly.

"No one can understand it," Miss Jones went on. "Apparently the Major was nowhere near the canteen when it happened."

After lunch – which was sandwiches in the hall – Class 3D gathered in the Design Technology Workshop to help convert Sam's wheelchair into a Monster Catcher.

Beth cut the girder and hinged it so that Sam could keep it upright like a flagpole when he wasn't actually catching monsters. The enormous reel of rope was fixed to the back of his chair.

"That will counter-balance the rod," said Beth. "So he doesn't tip forwards."

As she was speaking, Sam's wheelchair tipped backwards.

"Well, it will work when you're using the rod," Beth told Sam.

"This is fine," said Sam. "I can do wheelies." He demonstrated – and smacked straight into the wall.

A massive steel girder stuck up from the front of Sam's wheelchair, hinged and bent and attached to a rope. The rope looped round the chair and on to the enormous drum welded to the back of Sam's seat.

If the Chaplain noticed these adjustments to Sam's wheelchair, he didn't mention it. Sam waited with the others as the Chaplain explained what they were doing today in PE.

"And whatever you do, avoid the landmines," the Chaplain was saying. "Any questions?"

Alfie stuck his hand up. "Can we just run round the lake instead, sir?"

The Chaplain's eyes narrowed. "Run round the lake?"

"Oh yes, please, sir," said Beth.

"Is that dangerous?" the Chaplain asked.

"Er, could be. Quite dangerous," said Jack.

"Doesn't sound very dangerous. I think we'll stick to the land-mines, barbed wire and exploding Space Hoppers."

"There's a monster," said Alfie. "That's quite dangerous. More dangerous than barbed wire. Probably."

"A monster?" the Chaplain didn't sound very convinced.

"And a giant duck," Harry said.

"Though not any more," Jack pointed out. "Sorry, Alice."

"We could put land-mines on the path round the lake," Chloe suggested. "And barbed wire."

"So long as we don't hurt any fish," Alice added.

"Well, I'm not sure," the Chaplain said. "I was going to surprise you with an automated artillery barrage behind the bike sheds."

Sam sighed. "I'll never get to catch the monster now."

"*Catch* the monster?" the Chaplain was astounded. "You were actually going to try to catch this enormous, dangerous monster you say is in the lake?"

"With Sam's wheelchair," said Alfie.

"Specially modified to make it into a Monster Catcher," said Beth proudly.

The Chaplain inspected Sam's wheelchair. He prodded at the girder, and for some reason kicked the wheelchair tyres.

"What you suggest is appallingly dangerous and you must all be completely mad," said the Chaplain. "Let's do it!"

"Right then," said the Chaplain as they gathered on the path by the lake. "What are you using for bait?"

"Bait?" said Beth.

"We didn't use bait at Fishing Club," said Alfie "I think we do that bit next week."

"Got to have bait," said the Chaplain. "Can't catch monsters without bait. So I'll need a volunteer."

"To go and get the bait?" Jack asked.

The Chaplain glared at him. "To *be* the bait. Monsters probably eat school children. I would if I were a monster."

"I volunteer Alfie to be the bait," said Chloe.

"Good idea. Tie him to the rope," the Chaplain decided.

"Er," said Alfie. "Couldn't we just tie a loop in the end of the rope? Like a lasso?"

The Chaplain frowned. "Doesn't sound very dangerous," he said.

Which, oddly, was why it appealed to Alfie.

After three circuits of the lake, Alfie was getting out of breath. He was not sure they really needed the added incentive of a pack of Hungarian attack dogs chasing after them. But at least he wasn't swimming monster bait.

One of the dogs behind him took a corner too quickly and shot over the edge of the bank, landing in the lake with a splash. Another leaped at Jack, who quickened his pace. Beth was out in front – but Alfie reckoned she was

cheating by wearing rocket-boosted wheelie-trainers. They worked very well, except when she hit a bump in the path and shot ten metres up in the air.

Sam was moving slowly in his wheelchair.

The girder was extended in front of him so he looked like a crane. The rope was trailing in the water as Sam moved, trying to get the monster to bite. The dogs were ignoring Sam now, after several of them had broken their teeth on the metal of his chair.

"No sign of the monster yet," Sam reported as Alfie raced past.

"What about the..." Alfie had to pause to take a gulp of air.

"Duck," the Chaplain shouted.

"Yes," Alfie said. "The— waaaa-ouff!" The trailing rope from Sam's Monster Catcher rod hit Alfie on the head and sent him sprawling.

"Told you to duck," said the Chaplain.

"Sorry, Alfie." Sam was grinning. But the grin seemed to freeze on his face as his wheelchair suddenly lurched and then shot forward at high speed.

Everyone stopped to watch in amazement as Sam went racing down the path. Even the Hungarian attack dogs. The rope was taut, dragging him rapidly along. Sam's baseball cap flew off and his chair tilted backwards. The girder was bending under the strain.

"I think Sam's caught the monster," said Harry.

"I think the monster's caught Sam," Alfie told him.

With a crack like a gunshot, the rope

snapped. Sam kept going in the direction he was already heading – straight for an oak tree at the side of the lake. Alfie and the others closed their eyes at the moment of impact.

When they looked back, Sam was lying in a heap next to his toppled wheelchair. They all ran to help.

"I'm all right," Sam assured them. "Anyone seen my cap?"

"Haven't even seen the duck," Beth complained. "Let alone the monster."

"If there is one," Chloe muttered.

Alfie said nothing. He was disappointed they hadn't seen anything, and he was beginning to wonder if the monster had just been a trick of the light. But he was *sure* he'd seen it.

"Sorry," the Chaplain told everyone as he

hurried to join them, "but I still don't think it was dangerous."

"It seemed pretty dangerous to me," said the oak tree.

Chapter 5

It was break straight after PE. Beth took Sam off to remove the Monster Catcher from his wheelchair and straighten his wheels. Alice went to help.

"That was useless," said Chloe. "I blame Alfie for not being bait."

Alfie felt a bit upset that she thought it was his fault that Sam had nearly got hurt. But he didn't say anything.

"Well, we know there's something in the

lake now," said Jack.

"Maybe it really is a monster," Alfie suggested.

"Might have been the duck," said Harry.

Chloe wasn't impressed. "An underwater duck?"

"With flippers and goggles," said Jack. "Could be. There's something fishy in there."

"A fish?" Harry suggested.

"Lots of them, I expect," Alfie told him. "That's why we have the Fishing Club here, after all."

"After all what?" Harry asked.

"After all the other lessons," said Jack. "At the end of the day. You know."

"So what do we do now?" Chloe wanted to know.

On the other side of the lake, Alfie could see Rod and Annette getting ready for Class 4A's Fishing Club. They were taking equipment out of a big bag. Funny, Alfie thought, he hadn't noticed them earlier.

"Haddock," Jack announced. "That's the answer."

"Er sorry, what's the question?" said Harry.

Was that a bottle Rod was holding? Alfie couldn't quite see, but it looked like Annette was pushing something into it and then Rod threw it in the water.

"Haddock live in the sea," Chloe was telling Jack.

"Specially trained rare freshwater haddock," Jack decided. "With little cameras strapped to them. We let them loose to hunt for the monster."

"And what if the monster eats them?" Chloe asked.

"Alice will get very upset," said Alfie. He'd given up trying to see what Rod and Annette were doing.

"Right," said Harry. "That's the plan then – don't tell Alice the haddock have been eaten."

"I like the idea of a fish," Alfie agreed as they walked

back up to the school.

"I can swim as well as a fish," said Chloe. "I won all the races we had when we did swimming in PE last year."

"We all won," Jack reminded her. "If you didn't win, you got eaten by the shark."

"Or crushed by the octopus," Harry added.

"Well, I came first out of the winners," said Chloe.

"So what's your plan, Alfie?" Jack asked.

Alfie wasn't really sure. He'd just been thinking out loud. "I don't know. Maybe there is some way we can *make* a fish. Perhaps Beth can build an electric one that we can remote control or something. But I'm not sure electricity and water go well together. It might not work in water."

"Do electric eels stop working then?" Harry wondered.

"It might be easier," Alfie went on, "just to disguise one of us as a fish. Then the monster won't get suspicious."

"Might eat them though," said Jack.

"So," Harry asked brightly, "who is the best swimmer in the class?"

They all looked at Chloe.

"I won all the swimming in PE last year," she said. "But that was before Alfie joined the class. I bet he's the best swimmer of us all really."

Alfie was beginning to think he might have done better to say nothing.

By the end of the next day's Design Technology lesson, Alfie was sure he should have said

nothing. Beth, Sam and Alice had all loved the plan – which was somehow now all Chloe's idea – to disguise Alfie as a fish. Alfie became more and more anxious as the lesson went on...

Everyone else was very excited as they spent the lesson designing and building what Beth called a Special Aqua-Ready Disguise Involving New Equipment. Or SARDINE for short.

It was built around an old-fashioned diver's

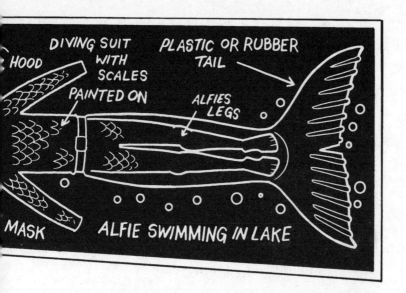

DIVING SUIT
WITH
SCALES
PAINTED ON

HOOD

PLASTIC OR RUBBER
TAIL

ALFIES
LEGS

MASK

ALFIE SWIMMING IN LAKE

wet suit. With scales painted along the body, and a specially made tail added it did look quite like a fish. Except for Alfie's head poking out the other end, complete with goggles and a small underwater camera.

"I still think we should have given the camera to a haddock," Jack complained.

"Fish don't have cameras," Beth told him. "They can't work the flash."

"I'm not sure fish have oxygen tanks strapped to their back either," Alice said.

"They might," said Beth. "If they want to be safe."

"We need to make a head for the fish now," said Jack. "Any ideas, Beth?"

"Maybe Alfie can just open and close his mouth a bit, like a goldfish."

"Big goldfish," said Chloe. "Though Alfie does look ugly enough to be a fish."

"If he swims really fast, no one will have time to see he's not a fish," Sam said.

"Do fish know what other fish look like?" Harry wondered.

No one was quite sure about this. "I suppose the other fish might just think Alfie is a funny big fish or something," said Jack. "Nice one, Harry."

"Or," said Alfie quietly, "they might think I'm some kid dressed in a painted wet suit with a plastic tail."

"Don't worry," Beth told him. "It's what the monster thinks that matters."

"And whether you're a boy or a fish," said Jack with a grin, "you might still make a great lunch."

They decided to launch Alfie in afternoon break. That way he'd be able to search the lake for the monster before the after-school Fishing Club. Class 3D gathered at the lakeside, while Alfie struggled into the wet suit and Beth attached his tail.

"I hope the paint's waterproof," she said.

"Bit late to worry about it now," Jack told her.

"Are those oxygen tanks fitted securely?"

Sam positioned himself at the top of a slope down to the edge of the lake. Jack and Harry lifted Alfie up and laid him sideways across the arms of Sam's wheelchair.

"Can't I just sort of jump in or something?" Alfie asked. "Walk, maybe? Well, sort of wiggle in on my tail anyway."

"Better this way," Sam assured him. "More fun."

"Yes – but who for?" Alfie asked. No one heard him though, as the wheelchair was already accelerating down the slope. It went faster and faster. The edge of the lake seemed to hurtle towards Alfie, though in fact he was hurtling towards it. Then Sam applied his Inertia-Cancelling Brake Mode, and the

wheelchair stopped.

Alfie didn't. He kept going at high speed –
through the air and out over the lake.

Then he was falling, splashing into the cold,

murky water, and struggling to get his breathing tube in place. He felt frightened and alone – even without worrying if he was going to be eaten by a huge monster.

Once he had sorted out his breathing, Alfie actually found it quite relaxing under the water. It was a strange, silent world. He soon worked

out how to wiggle his legs so his tail propelled him along. He could see a few metres ahead as he swam.

There were lots of curious fish, and all sorts of strange objects lying on the bed of the lake. In amongst the weed and the mud, Alfie saw an old boot, several plastic bags, a bicycle wheel,

a garden gnome, and an abandoned shopping trolley.

Alfie lost track of how long he was down there. His oxygen gauge was over half empty when he decided it was time to find the bank and report back to the others that he had found nothing.

Then, as he turned, he saw the monster.

It loomed at him out of the water. Alfie's stomach did a flip-flop as a great, bulbous nose nudged him aside. Then a huge, grey body slid past him. A large fin stuck out from the side, and the water behind the monster was churning and white with bubbles. Alfie was struggling to breathe as he watched the monster go past.

Despite being very frightened, Alfie remembered to use the camera attached to his

face mask. He wasn't sure whether the pictures would be any good, or even if they would come out. But he had other things to worry about – like swimming away as fast as he could before the monster spotted him.

Suddenly, Alfie felt a sharp pain at the back of his neck. The next thing he knew he was being dragged backwards through the water so fast he felt his stomach do a back flip.

Chapter 6

As he was speeding backwards through the water, Alfie grabbed desperately at anything he could reach to try to stop himself. The shopping trolley whizzed past, but he missed that. Handfuls of pondweed came away from the lake bed and his hand closed on something smooth and rounded.

Then he was flying through the air, and landing with a heavy thump on the bank beside a startled Harry. Who was holding a fishing rod.

Which had a line running from it to a large hook. Which was stuck through the back of Alfie's wet suit.

"What have you caught?" Jack asked.

"Er, Alfie," said Harry.

"Throw him back," Chloe told him.

"Thanks a lot," said Alfie. He spluttered and coughed and struggled to get his breath back.

But he was almost laughing with relief at being back on dry land.

"At least we know my Extra-Strength Automatic Recoil Fishing Reel works," Beth said.

"Sorry, Alfie," said Harry. "I was just getting in some extra practice while we waited."

Sam wheeled up, Alice close behind him. "Did you see the monster?" he wanted to know.

Alfie managed to detach the hook and line from the back of his neck. "Yes. And I think I got some pictures of it!"

"And what's that you're holding?" Jack asked.

Alfie looked at what he'd grabbed in the water. "An old bottle."

The last lesson of the day was Information

Technology. Instead of hacking into the United States Military Command computers, Miss Jones let Class 3D work on the digital photographs that Alfie had taken.

"Provided Alfie stops dripping on the floor and dries himself off," she added. "I think you can change back into your normal clothes now. And you'll find it easier to sit at your desk without that tail."

By the time Alfie got back, Beth had loaded the photos on to a computer and was projecting the results on to the classroom whiteboard.

"That's a fish," said Alice as the first picture came up.

"That's another fish," said Jack at the second one.

"Oh," Chloe said as the third picture flashed

up. "Guess what that is. A fish."

"Pondweed," said Beth to the fourth.

"And what is that?" Miss Jones asked as the next picture appeared.

"Oh we've studied those in Surveillance," said Sam. "It's a shopping trolley. Can be very dangerous."

"I think they've changed the way the wheels work now," said Miss Jones. "So they're not as dangerous as they used to be."

Harry was examining the old bottle that Alfie had found. "I think there's something inside it," he announced.

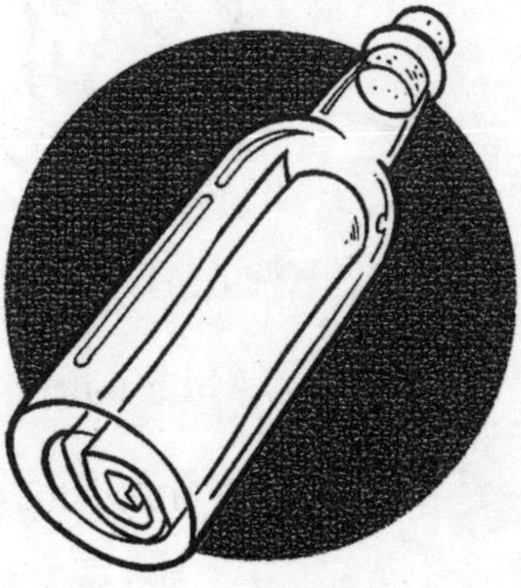

"Water, probably," Jack told him. "Don't drink it!"

"No, it's paper." Harry

unscrewed the top and managed to tease out the rolled up paper. "It's a note."

"What's it say?" Alfie asked. Harry handed him the note, and Alfie read it out: "'TO Agents A R. Usual RV after FC. Progress Report to H of S.'"

"Sounds like something Mr Cryption might say," Alice said.

"Let me see that." Jack took the note and

inspected it. "Of course. We just need to work out the letters. What this means is: 'Throw Out Agents At River. Usual River Visit after Five o'clock.' So someone is going to throw some agents in the river and then go and see what's happened to them at five o'clock before reporting back to H of S. That'll be the Head of School – Mr Trenchard."

Miss Jones took the note from Jack. "I'm not sure it's about Mr Trenchard at all. I'll go and get him. He'll want to see this."

"Why do you think he'd be interested?" Sam asked after Miss Jones had left.

"Maybe," Alfie suggested, "because the message could be addressed to Agents Annette and Rod, telling them there's the usual rendezvous after Fishing Club, and that they have to make a progress report to the Head of SPUD."

There was silence for a few moments, then Harry said, "You mean that Rod and Annette are working for SPUD?"

"Could be," said Jack.

"I did see them throw a bottle in the lake," Alfie told everyone. "Maybe they were sending a message."

"To the monster?" Chloe asked. "Get real."

"This looks real," Beth said. She had moved on to the next photo. It showed a large, grey, bulbous shape. "But I don't think it's a monster."

The next photo showed the fin – which looked like it was made of metal.

Another photo showed the tail end of the monster. Only it wasn't a tail at all.

Mr Trenchard arrived in time to see the photo appear on the whiteboard. "Good gracious, where was that picture taken?"

"In the lake," Alfie explained.

"Our lake? Here at Thunder Raker Manor?"

"What is it, Mr Trenchard?" Alice asked.

"It's the back end of a new submarine that SPUD has been developing specially for operations in shallow water."

"A SPUDmarine!" said Sam.

"That's right. They can hide agents inside it and keep watch. While they're on duty," Mr Trenchard said, "they all live in a shallow SPUDmarine."

"A shallow SPUDmarine?" everyone echoed.

"A shallow SPUDmarine," Mr Trenchard agreed. "They all live in… But never mind that now. This is very serious if we have SPUD agents hidden in the lake. They must be spying on Thunder Raker."

"We think they've infiltrated the Fishing Club," said Jack.

"Goodness," said Mr Trenchard. "Do we have a Fishing Club? Disguised themselves as bait or something have they?"

"It's Rod Boiled and Annette Mash who run the club," Alfie explained. "They must be working for SPUD."

"Good work." Mr Trenchard turned to Miss Jones. "We have to sort this out at once. I'm giving the mission of stopping the SPUDmarine and getting rid of these dastardly agents to Class 3D. It can count as coursework towards their SATS."

Chapter 7

Homework that night was to come up with a plan to capture the SPUDmarine.

"That's nice," said Alfie's mum when he told her all about it. "You let me know if you need any help, won't you."

"Thanks, Mum."

"And don't forget to underline the heading and put your name on it."

Alfie's dad was watching television. "I hope you kept the bottle you found that message in.

The secret is to force the submarine to surface so you can get on board," he said. "I expect. Not that I've ever done anything like that myself. Not for years. Not since... I wonder if there's anything good on the Golf Channel?" he went on quickly.

Alfie thought this was a strange thing to say. His dad didn't even like golf. But he had a few ideas now, and soon finished his homework.

When Alfie arrived for school the next morning, everyone else was already in the classroom.

"Jack's got a plan," Beth explained.

Everyone waited excitedly as one arm of Sam's wheelchair opened. A rod extended upwards and rolled up paper unfurled from it like a flag. On the paper was a picture.

"That's a badger," said Alice. "Again."

"Not just any old badger," explained Jack.

"Why's it got that thing on its head?" Chloe wanted to know.

"This is a SUB," said Jack. "And we use it as a key element of SICK in our BUCKET."

There was silence for a moment. Then Harry said, "It just looks like a badger to me."

Jack sighed. "That's what I just said."

"Do you think you could say it again, please?" asked Alfie. "I'm not sure I quite understood."

"It's very easy." Jack pointed at the picture. "This is our SUB, and we use it—"

"Hang on, hang on," Beth told him. "SUB? As in 'submarine'?"

"Special Underwater Badger."

Sam nodded knowingly. "That'll be why it's wearing scuba-diving kit then."

"Exactly."

"And it has to be sick in a bucket?" asked Harry.

Jack stared at him. "What are you talking about?"

"No," Chloe said to Jack, "what are *you* talking about?"

"It's the sick-in-a-bucket bit we're having problems with now," explained Alfie. "Tell us your plan again, Jack," he suggested. "Without the initials this time. Just spell it all out."

Jack took a deep breath. "Special Underwater Badger," he said, pointing to the picture. "Part of SICK – er, that's our Submarine Identification and Capture Kit in our BUCKET. I mean, our Brilliant Underwater Capture Kit Executive Task."

"Does that actually make sense?" Chloe asked.

"Maybe not, but it makes BUCKET."

"So what exactly *is* the plan?" Beth wanted to know.

"And what else is in this SICK kit?" Sam asked.

"Well, obviously," Jack told them, "the underwater badgers will need a tin opener."

"Need a what?" Alfie asked.

"A tin opener."

"Why?"

"It's simple, right?" said Jack. "The Special Underwater Badgers locate the SPUDmarine, OK? Then they hack their way in with a tin opener. The SPUDmarine starts leaking and it sinks."

"I thought submarines were supposed to sink," Harry said. "Isn't that the idea?"

"Yes, but this one will *sink* sink. You see?"

"No," said Harry.

"And," Beth added, "we don't have any badgers."

Jack folded his arms. "Well, if anyone's got a better plan, let's hear it."

"You mean one with fewer badgers?" said Alice.

Alfie looked around, but no one else seemed ready to say anything else.

"Yes, Alfie?" Beth asked.

"I was just thinking," said Alfie, remembering what his dad had told him, "that we need the SPUDmarine to come to the surface, not to sink. Then we can get on board."

"It's a submarine," Chloe said. "How do we get them to come to the surface?"

"We could send them a letter," Alfie said.

Harry put his hand up. "Wouldn't it get a bit soggy?"

Sam nodded. "Be very difficult to read. The ink would run, and everything."

"Not if we put it in a bottle. That's how Rod and Annette keep in touch with the agents in the SPUDmarine."

"Good one, Alfie," said Beth. "And we've got their bottle already, so we can use that."

Alice was keen too. "Rod and Annette didn't get the last message from the SPUDmarine because we found it first. We could send a message back *to* the SPUDmarine that seems to come from them and arrange another meeting."

"Only *we'll* be there waiting," Jack agreed. "With our badgers and tin opener."

"The Chaplain's got some depth-charges," said Chloe. "He uses them in Lower 2nd swimming lessons, I've heard. They might be useful."

"And we should get the Major involved," Sam said.

"And Sergeant Custer," said Alice.

Harry nodded. "And Gerald."

"Good plan, Alfie," said Beth.

"Only *bits* of it were Alfie's," Chloe grumbled.

But Alfie didn't mind. He was looking forward to capturing the SPUDmarine.

Chapter 8

Jack did the first draft of the letter to send to the SPUDmarine. He read it out proudly to everyone:

Dear SPUD Agents, I hope you are
well. Rod and Annette asked me to
write to you to ask you to meet them
at the edge of the lake by the
weeping willow tree — you know that
one with the dippy branches that
bend into the water — tomorrow
evening after Fishing Club.

Many thanks.

Yours sincerely
Class 3D
PS — This is not a trap. Really.

"Well," said Jack, "what do you think?"

Chloe shook her head sadly. "You have no idea, have you?"

"What?"

"How long have you been at this school?" she demanded. "How long have you been learning all about Undercover Agent Work, Secret Messages, Sabotage Training, Maths and English?"

"What's the problem?"

Chloe was exasperated. "You honestly don't know? Are you *so* stupid? Do I really have to tell you?" She sighed. "In a letter like that, where you don't know the name of the person you're sending it to, you finish 'Yours faithfully', not 'Yours sincerely'."

"Um," Alfie said, "there are a couple of other things we might want to change too, I think."

"Really?" said Harry. "I thought it was good."

"Thanks, Harry," said Jack.

"Oh it's great," Alfie said quickly. "But if we're changing it anyway, I just wonder whether it would be less suspicious if it wasn't signed as coming from Class 3D."

"Well doh," Jack said. "I wasn't going to sign it 'Jack' was I? That would be a dead give-away."

"I know," Alice said. "Why don't we make it seem like it *actually* came from Rod and Annette?"

"Brilliant!" Sam said. "Why didn't you think of that, Alfie?"

Alfie had thought of that. In fact, he thought that was the plan. But he said nothing.

Jack was busy crossing out 'Yours sincerely, Class 3D' and writing 'Yours faithfully, Rod and Annette'.

"I suppose," Alfie said slowly, "we could make it a bit more like the message we found as well. That might help fool them."

"Oh yes!" Beth agreed. "Let's see that original message."

Soon they had a new message that everyone was happy with. It said:

```
FROM Agents A R. RV after FC by
willow tree. Progress Report ready
for H of S.
```

Jack wanted to keep the 'PS – This is not a trap' but everyone else managed to persuade him it wasn't needed.

Harry put the message inside the bottle Alfie had found. "How do we get it to the SPUDmarine?"

"I saw where Rod and Annette threw a bottle into the water," Alfie said. "We can just throw this in at the same place. The SPUDmarine must be keeping a look out."

"But what if Rod and Annette are there?" said Harry.

"They will be," said Chloe. "We're pretending to be them."

"No, I mean, what if they're *really* there. Really. In real life."

Alfie paused. "Good point. For all we know

they might be sending a message at the same time as us. We need a way to get rid of them…"

The Fishing Club was just finishing when Rod and Annette were surprised to see a frail figure coming towards them. The little old lady seemed quite doddery and picked her way very carefully down the slope towards the lake.

It was a bit odd that the children who were leaving the Fishing Club kept so far away from her. Not one of them went to help the old lady, though she said good afternoon to them, and waved her walking stick in a friendly way.

"Can I help you?" Rod asked as the old lady approached.

"You are so very kind," she said in a cracked voice.

"This is Rod and I'm Annette. We run the Fishing Club," Annette explained.

"My name is Miss Fortune," said the little old lady.

Rod reached out to shake hands. "I'm very pleased to— oof!"

Annette watched in surprise as the old lady grabbed Rod's hand and flipped him expertly through the air. Before she could react, Annette found herself grabbed in an advanced judo hold. Then she was flying after Rod, a Korean karate victory cry echoing in her ears. She smacked into an oak tree and slid to the ground, dazed.

"Oof!" said the oak tree.

The frail little old lady continued on her hesitant walk round the lake.

Alfie and his friends watched from behind the hanging branches of the weeping willow a short distance away.

"So far so good," said Jack.

"All going according to plan," Beth agreed.

The next part of the plan involved Alfie and Chloe, though Chloe wasn't too happy about it. But she was the most like Annette, and Alfie was the most like Rod. Though they were both smaller.

They ran over to where the school nurse was now tending to Rod and Annette. Both were lying unconscious, and Nurse Deadman tied

them up in bandages so they couldn't escape.

"I'll give them an aspirin each and they'll be fine," she told Alfie.

"That's her cure for everything," Chloe whispered. "Beth broke her leg a couple of years ago testing a jet pack. Nurse Deadman gave her an aspirin. It was the same after that nasty accident on the school minefield..."

Alfie and Chloe took the dark glasses from Rod and Annette and put them on.

"You look well cool," Alfie told Chloe.

She smiled. Then she seemed to realise she

didn't want to smile, and tried to stop. "Yes," she said. "I do. Always."

"Right," Alfie said quickly, "let's go and stand by the willow tree and pretend to be Rod and Annette waiting for the meeting with the SPUDmarine."

"They'll be fooled by *me*," Chloe said. "I look every bit as glamorous as Annette. But Rod's quite handsome. You'd better stay back in the shadows."

Behind them, Nurse Deadman was dragging the real Rod and Annette away on one of the school dinner trolleys. Rod was complaining in a dazed way, because he was on the bottom shelf.

In their hiding place under the willow tree, the rest of Class 3D watched and waited. A few other people had joined them now, slipping carefully and *almost* silently into hiding.

"Oops, sorry – was that your leg?" said one of them.

"Woof," said another.

"Quiet, Gerald," a third voice hissed.

"When I was in the Royal Horse Artillery we had savage attack gerbils that could rip a man's arm off," another voice said.

"What – not horses?" someone answered. It sounded like Harry.

But Alfie wasn't listening. He was watching the massive, dark shape of a submarine rising majestically from the lake in front of him. The whole of the bulbous nose swung open to reveal the dark interior. A figure stepped out – a man wearing a dark suit and even darker glasses.

"Is that you, Rod?" the man called out.

"Only that doesn't look much like Annette with you."

"He must be blind," said Chloe. "It'll be those dark glasses they all wear."

Chapter 9

The SPUDmarine was still a way out into the lake. The SPUD agent had to wade waist-deep in water to get to the shore. As soon as he reached the edge of the lake, lots of things happened.

First, he saw that not only was Annette not really Annette, but also that Rod wasn't really Rod either. His mouth dropped open in surprise, and he turned to run.

But before he could get back to the

SPUDmarine, Gerald the guard dog bounded from under the willow tree and launched himself at the unfortunate SPUD agent. The man was knocked into the water with a cry.

"Well done, Gerald," Sergeant Custer called as he ran after his dog. The Major and the Chaplain were close behind, with Class 3D following. The Chaplain tripped on something and went flying.

"Oops," said the Major. "Sorry, Chaplain."

But the Chaplain managed to turn his fall into an impressive dive into the water. He swam the short distance to the open hatch at the front of the SPUDmarine and pulled himself inside.

"Come on!" the Chaplain yelled at everyone else. "Last one in gets to feed the school panther. He likes children."

More SPUD agents in suits and dark glasses were appearing in the open hatchway. When they saw the Chaplain, dripping with lake water and flexing his muscles, they ran back inside the SPUDmarine.

The Chaplain followed. His voice echoed back to where Alfie was wading through the water with Jack.

"Right, you horrible load of SPUDs, let's be having you. You – yes, *you!* – on the floor now. Press-ups. I want to see a hundred, quick as you can or I'll have you mucking out the tiger enclosure with a toothbrush. One-two-one-two... Right the way up now, no cheating."

"I don't think they stand a chance," said Jack.

"Slowcoaches!" Sam cried as he went past. His wheelchair was supported on large

florescent orange inflatable floats. There
was a propeller at the back.

"Beth fixed it up for him," Jack explained.
"He didn't want to miss the fun."

Beth was close behind Sam – hanging on to
the back of the wheelchair by a rope, and
skimming over the lake on water-skis. She
waved, wobbled, and was gone.

On the other side of Jack, the Major waded
quickly through the water. "Soon be there," he
proclaimed. "Unless there's any— glug glug."

He seemed to vanish from view suddenly, leaving only bubbles bursting on the surface of the lake.

By the time Alfie and Jack arrived at the SPUDmarine, lots of SPUD agents were leaving it. They were swimming then wading to the edge of the lake. Where a kindly looking old lady was waiting to help them ashore.

Inside, the SPUDmarine seemed very cramped. It was lit with red emergency lighting and there was a siren going off. Alfie could hear the Chaplain shouting orders somewhere deep inside.

Harry was standing beside a SPUD agent who was cowering on the floor. Harry was holding a cricket bat. As Alfie watched, Harry

turned the cricket bat round and pushed the handle gently towards the SPUD agent.

"Here you are," said Harry.

"What are you doing?" Alfie asked.

"Oh, hi, Alfie." Harry held up the cricket bat again. "The Chaplain said to let him have it. But he doesn't seem to want it."

Sam was whizzing down the corridor on his wheelchair. "We got most of them," he said. "But some SPUD agents have locked themselves in the control room."

"Gangway!" a voice shouted from behind them. The Major came barrelling through, dripping wet. "Locked themselves in the control room, eh? I'll soon sort them out."

His shoulder caught on a large valve attached to a pipe near the low ceiling. The valve tore away and water poured out.

"Sorry!" the Major said as he kept going. His foot snagged on a cable, wrenching it from its socket. Sparks shot across the corridor. The SPUDmarine lurched to one side, sending the Major tumbling through an open hatch.

"Woah!"

Alfie ran after the Major. There was a man-sized, Major-shaped hole in the wall, and through it, Alfie could see the startled SPUD agents in the main control room. The Major was bouncing off the control panels. He tried to grab things to steady himself, but whatever he touched seemed to fall to bits or explode.

"Oops… Sorry…" said the Major. A pipe came apart and water sprayed everywhere. "Was that me? Sorry." The SPUDmarine's periscope collapsed in a shattering mess of

metal and glass. "I should get that looked at, if I were you…"

"Evacuate!" a SPUD agent yelled above the sound of sirens and explosions and the Chaplain's booming voice.

The Major was carried along with the flow of SPUD agents as they raced for the exit. Alfie

leaped to one side to avoid being knocked flying. He saw Chloe, Alice, and Jack run past too. Alfie was about to follow everyone else when he saw a monitor screen nearby.

On the screen was an image of a large black rat. It was sitting on a desk, and there was a figure seated behind the desk, but Alfie couldn't see who. A white-gloved hand stroked the rat's head. Another offered it a bit of carrot.

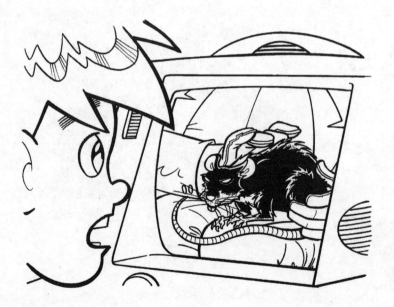

"What is going on, there?" said the man stroking the rat. "Captain Dauphinoise – what's happening?"

It was a voice that Alfie recognised. It was the Head of SPUD.

Then the same voice went on, "I'm sorry, sir. It looks like we have lost contact."

Sir?! Who did the Head of SPUD call 'sir'? Was there someone even more important?

Alfie soon had his answer. He gaped with astonishment as the large black rat said, "So it would seem." Its voice was shrill and angry. Its dark eyes peered at the monitor screen. Then the rat said, "I've seen that boy before. Who are you?" it demanded, staring unmistakably at Alfie.

The Head of SPUD was a rat!

Alfie didn't answer. He backed away. Then the screen blanked out and suddenly everything went pitch black.

"Ah, sorry," the Major's voice echoed round the dark SPUDmarine. "Think that might have been me."

The Chaplain's voice was even louder. "Everyone out! The sub's sinking!" There was a pause, then, "Yes, Harry I know that's what submarines do, but this time it's a bit of a problem. Last one out gets to test the hand-grenades."

Alfie could hear the sound of rushing water. He could feel his legs getting wet as the water rose. Finally, the red lights came back on, and he saw that water was pouring out of broken pipes all round him. It was now up to his waist.

At the back of the control room, two SPUD agents were working frantically at the controls. "It's no good. Abandon ship!" said one.

"We'll have to use the camouflaged escape capsules," said the other.

The way that Alfie had come in was blocked by a fallen girder. He had no idea how to find the way out, so he followed the SPUD agents –

they must know their way round.

In the corridor ahead of him, Alfie saw the
SPUD agents standing by a door. The woman
pressed a button and the door opened. They
hurried inside.

Sloshing through the rising water, Alfie
followed. He heard a whoosh from behind
the door and through a hatch he saw

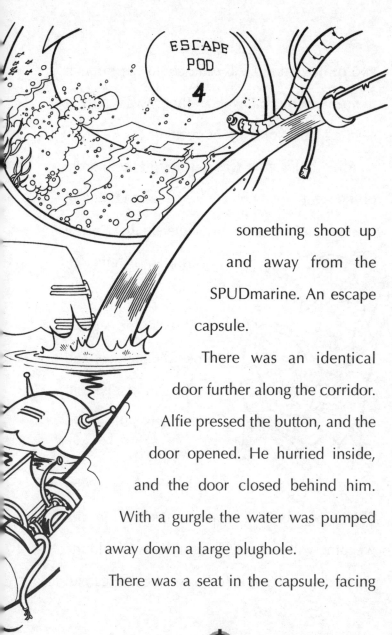

ESCAPE POD

4

something shoot up
and away from the
SPUDmarine. An escape
capsule.

There was an identical
door further along the corridor.
Alfie pressed the button, and the
door opened. He hurried inside,
and the door closed behind him.
With a gurgle the water was pumped
away down a large plughole.

There was a seat in the capsule, facing

two oval windows. All Alfie could see through them was murky water. There was also a steering wheel and a foot pedal.

A big red button was flashing in the middle of the steering wheel. Alfie pressed the button.

Immediately there was a whoosh, and Alfie felt himself pressed into the seat. The escape capsule broke the surface, and Alfie could see out through the two windows.

He could see the Chaplain organising the SPUD agents to do press-ups beside the weeping willow tree. He could see Gerald the guard dog and Sergeant Custer keeping careful

watch. He could see his friends from Class 3D safely ashore. Jack and Alice were helping the Major out of the water.

And right in front of him, speeding away in the opposite direction, Alfie could see the most enormous bright yellow duck.

Chapter 10

On the bank, Harry dived to the ground. Jack shook his head, pointing across the lake. He was pointing at the yellow duck. Then he was pointing at Alfie.

That was when Alfie realised that he was inside another duck. He leaned forward to peer through the windows, and saw that they were the eyes of the duck. A large red beak jutted out beneath them. The yellow duck streaking away across the lake must be the other escape capsule – and the two SPUD agents were escaping in it.

Alfie pushed his foot down on the pedal, and felt his duck accelerate across the lake. It took him a while to get the hang of the steering. He whooshed close to the edge of the lake, sending a wave of water splashing across class 3D as he turned.

They could all see Alfie through the duck's eyes. He could see Chloe – drenched from head to foot – pointing at the duck. "Alfie!" he could see her mouthing angrily. Beth and Jack were jumping up and down with excitement. Sam gave a dripping thumbs-up. Alice waved.

Alfie grinned and waved back.

Then he turned his duck towards the other one and set off in pursuit.

Alfie's duck was gaining on the SPUD duck. But he wasn't going fast enough to catch it before it reached the far side of the lake. Alfie expected the duck to turn or stop. But it didn't do either. It kept going – skimming up the bank and on to the school playing fields like a hovercraft.

Bracing himself, Alfie followed. His duck bumped up over the edge of the lake and after the SPUD duck.

There was a crackling noise from somewhere nearby, and Alfie realised it was a radio. A distorted voice echoed round the inside of the duck: "Beth to Alfie duck, Beth to Alfie duck. Can you hear me? Quack once for yes, and twice for no."

"Quack," Alfie shouted.

"He can hear me!" he heard Beth exclaim. "He's quacking."

"I think you're great too, Beth," said Alfie.

"The duck can speak!" Harry yelled.

"Of course it can. It's me, Alfie."

"Alfie's a duck?!" Harry gasped.

"Escape capsule duck," Alfie explained. "Must be a disguise, so if anyone saw an escape capsule in the distance, like we did, they'd think it was just a duck."

"Big duck," Sam's voice crackled. "No, Harry – get up."

"You probably couldn't tell the size if it was a long way away," Alice said. "I hope it didn't scare the fish."

"Who's the other duck?" Chloe asked.

"SPUD agents," Alfie explained.

"SPUD's agents are ducks?"

"No, Harry," Alfie said. "But their head is a rat."

"A duck with the head of a rat?!"

"Never mind. I'm gaining on their duck, but what do I do when I catch it?"

"Help's on its way," said Beth. "You should reach her any moment."

"Reach who?" Alfie asked.

But even as he spoke, he saw a little old lady with a walking stick step out from the trees at the edge of the playing field – right in front of the SPUD duck.

The duck skidded and turned desperately. But it was still heading for the old lady. She threw aside her walking stick and drew herself up to her full, unimpressive, height.

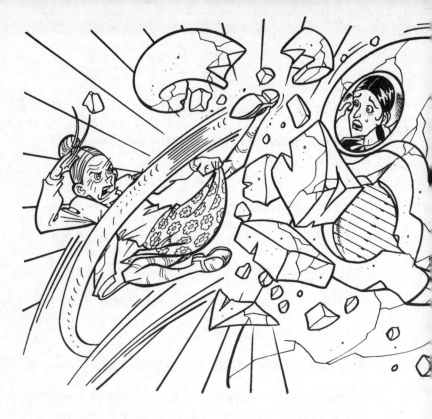

Then Miss Fortune leaped two metres into
the air. Her leg shot out in a perfectly timed
roundhouse kick. She seemed to hang in
space, leg extended. The kick connected with
the duck's beak. She followed through with
the other foot before landing in front of the
duck. Clenched fists lashed out.

The duck's beak crumpled. It toppled over on its side.

Alfie brought his own duck to a stop close behind the stricken SPUD duck. He pushed open the hatch in the side and climbed carefully out.

"It's all right, it's me – Alfie."

Miss Fortune regarded him through flint-hard narrowed eyes. Then she stooped awkwardly to pick up her walking stick and hobbled away. She paused only to say, "Good afternoon, young man," in a frail, cracked voice.

Next day, there was a special assembly. Mr Trenchard told the whole school about the SPUDmarine and how Class 3D had organised the operation to find and capture it.

Behind him, the other teachers were all listening carefully. The Chaplain was looking

very pleased with himself, and the Major had one arm in a sling and a sticking plaster across his forehead. The stage in front of him seemed to have a large crack across it. Next to the Major, at the side of the stage, was the usual empty chair.

"The SPUDmarine has now been recovered from the lake," Mr Trenchard said, "and sent for analysis to the Government Inventing Taskforce."

"GIT," said Mrs Nuffink.

"Indeed," Mr Trenchard agreed. "Thanks to the heroic efforts of Class 3D, we have also captured several SPUD agents, including Rod Boiled and Annette Mash. They are protesting their innocence, of course. Rod says it's all lies, but we don't think he's telling the truth."

Mr Cryption cleared his throat. "Warthog bathtub constellation shed?"

"Ah yes, I was coming to that. Thank you for reminding me. The captured SPUD agents have been sent for questioning to the Special Place for Interrogating Captives, and their stories will later be passed on to the Special Place for Analysing Narratives."

"SPIC and SPAN," said the Chaplain.

"Absolutely," Mr Trenchard agreed. "And neat and tidy and all sorted out. So it just remains for me to thank Class 3D formerly and present them with their certificate of thanks for Delivering an Underwater Knockout."

"DUK," said the Major.

"Get up, Harry," said Alfie. "That isn't what he meant."

"And finally," Mr Trenchard went on," a word of thanks to Mr Trick for first alerting us to the problems in the school lake."

"You're welcome," said the empty chair at the side of the stage.

READ ON FOR LOADS OF EXTRA CONTENT

Become a Secret Agent

Use this badge to fill in your secret agent details, but remember to keep it somewhere secret (like inside your sock) or other spies might find it. You never know who's watching you!

You can copy or trace the badge, or if you have a printer, go to www.harpercollins.co.uk/Contents/Author/JustinRichards/Pages/secret_Agent.aspx?objId=40653 to print it out.

Your secret agent name is the name of the first street you lived on, so if you lived on Greenhill Lane you would be Agent Greenhill. Your agent code is your age, plus your house number, plus how many brothers and sisters you have. So if your house number is three, you are eight years old and you have two brothers, your number would
be 13.

TIP! Cover your card in sellotape so it doesn't get wet when you're spying in wet conditions.

AGENT ALFIE

Stick a picture of yourself here

AGENT NAME......................................

AGENT CODE......................................

COUNTRY......................................

ASSIGNMENT......................................

MR TRICK'S

CAMOUFLAGE HINTS AND TIPS

IN THIS SPECIAL APPENDIX, MR
TRICK SHARES HIS SECRETS OF HOW
TO REMAIN UNSEEN AND KEEP
WATCH WITHOUT SPUD AGENTS EVER
WORKING OUT THAT ALL THE TIME
YOU ARE IN FACT, ACTUALLY

Hedgehog Slab Illusion

Huh?

Well, Mr Cryption might seem to be talking rubbish, but in fact everything he says is in code. Here are some of the code words that Mr Cryption uses together with what they really mean – provided by the Government Rapid Analysis Decoding and Encryption Section (GRADES). Other words have not yet been deciphered – perhaps you can work them out?

You can also use the list to say things in code, like Mr Cryption. But be warned – if you do, no one will know what you are talking about!

Codeword	Meaning
Alert	Letter
Antelopes	Satellite
Anthology	Collection
Armada	Tricky
Artichoke	Watch out
Bananas	Tummy

Codeword	Meaning
Bath	Big tub of water
Bathtub	Lake
Binoculars	Colour
Blue	Difficult
Brackets	Hiding place
Bridges	Dangerous
Butter	Damaged
Cardigans	Success
Carpet	Unexpected
Casement	Enclosed frame
Cashflow	Expensive
Constellation	Interrogation
Crisis	Envelope
Dilemma	If
Doom	Clever
Enormous	Worked
Extraction	Code-breaking
Fester	No
Flammable	When
Flippers	Flippers
Frosting	Frosting
Garden	Talking

Codeword	Meaning
Geography	Need
Gherkin	Outstanding
Gold	Stay
Golf	Camouflage
Hamster	Teacher
Hat stand	Saucepan
Heart-shaped	Secret
Hedgehog	Quick
Igloo	Completely
Imposter	Blanket
Identity	In
Illusion	Code
Luggage	Responsibility
Mangle	Achievement
Marbles	Brains
Nightmare	Hoorah!
Office	Not good
Pest	Hiding
Phoenix	Again
Pig	Today
Quibble	Better
Rewind	Recover

Codeword Meaning

Codeword	Meaning
Rock	Circumstances
Safety	Pink
Scribble	Message Ends
Shakespeare	Muddled
Shed	Facility
Slab	Guide
Sleepwalker	Deception
Slingshot	Hurt
Submarine	After school
Tailor	Lessons
Talks	Delivery
Tiles	Letters
Under	Extremely
Vikings	Fake
Violin	Stringed musical instrument
Visible	Detention
Window	Under
Wobble	Badly
Xylophonics	Good morning
Zebra	Black and white striped animal like a horse
Zero	Netting